475

MAGIC NUMBER

MAGIC NUMBER

Written and Illustrated by

HAROLD GOODWIN

BRADBURY PRESS

Englewood Cliffs, New Jersey

00948

Library of Congress Catalog Card Number: 78-75609
Manufactured in the United States of America
First printing   13-545103-5

The text of this book is set in 14 point Granjon. The
illustrations are ink drawings, reproduced in line.

To Barbara and Georgiana

1
ENIGMA

"It's RAINING," said Toad. A trickle of cold water ran under the rock where he lived. He looked out at the dark day and then hopped into the downpour. Toad blinked in amazement. A few yards away the edge of the rain made a sharp line across some stone steps and went no farther. At the top of the steps a house and a stone terrace were bathed in bright sunshine.

On the terrace there was a mixed group of squabbling pets. A duck flapped her wings at a stolid brown dog who barred her way. "I'm going down there," she squawked.

"Nobody leaves the patio," he answered. "It's the first rule."

A black and white cat stared fixedly through the wall of falling water at some small wild animals who had joined Toad in the wet grass. Nearby, a family of wary hamsters watched her tail twitch. "Nobody leaves the patio," she murmured.

A lamb asked the duck, "Why don't you jump in the pool if you want to get wet?" The terrace, which the pets all called "the patio," surrounded a lily pool where they swam in hot weather. The duck turned on Lamb. "What do you know about it? Can't you see that someone is taking away our rain. Look at that toad out there. How do you know that he's not behind all this?"

Lamb's attention had wandered. Dog stretched out across the top of the steps. "No one leaves the patio," he repeated firmly and stared down with contempt at the animals in the garden.

A parrot who was chained to a perch in the shade of some tall trees at the other end of the terrace watched the downpour. "The rains are coming," she whispered. "Take to the trees, for soon the black caymans and anacondas will leave the river. There will be piranhas in the pool. Take care, take care."

The other pets didn't hear her because just then the house door opened and the owner of the house, terrace, pool and weedy garden came out to look at the rain. He was Doctor J. W. Ordley, D.V.M., an animal doctor who was working to teach animals to behave better. He had raised the dog and cat with the family of golden hamsters and fed them nothing but vitamin-enriched

soybean paste with added iron. They had learned not to fight, hunt or roam off the terrace. Dr. Ordley was still trying to teach the duck to hate water and the lamb to fight. He used all the newest methods and best equipment for his training and kept careful notes of everything that happened.

"A sun shower!" he exclaimed. "How lovely. I hope there will be a rainbow." He turned on a loud but tiny portable radio. "Let's see if we can get a weather report."

WHEN THE SHOWER PASSED, the soaked wild animals, suddenly aware of being out in daylight, scurried back to their holes. They feared they might be attacked by the dog, the cat or the doctor. So they hid and waited patiently for the safety of the night. They all knew that slugs would be out after the rain and each privately planned to visit a certain patch of overgrown flowers that crowded a wall at the back of the garden.

When at last the only light came dimly from the windows of the house, they stole out one by one and headed for the flower patch. It proved indeed to be alive with slugs. There were soft horned blobs everywhere. Light leaked through the dripping leaves of the shaking plants to shine briefly on wet fur or a black eye as the hungry eaters gorged—and grumbled at the crowds. A dark snake wound among the stems where mantises and spiders lurked. Skunks, moles and toads were jostled by a quick darting shrew who appeared and disappeared. A brown bat flitted over all.

As each hunter arrived to find others already there, a

gabble of voices rose and floated in the misty darkness.

"Watch out—that was my slug."

"No, dear."

"Did you see the rude way those pets stared today?"

"This damp is terrible for my rheumatism."

"I liked being out in daylight. Can I go out tomorrow?"

"Hush—eat your slugs. Here's a cricket."

The pace slowed as stomachs grew full. The eaters began to assemble in sociable groups and the talk turned to familiar topics.

"Those pets! They sleep in nice snug beds while we hide in damp holes. The rain doesn't even fall on them. Talk about injustice!"

"Holes are terrible for rheumatism."

"It's unfair."

"Mama, why can't we go up there on the terrace and use the pool?"

"The dog or the cat would kill you, dear."

"Oh."

The shrew climbed on a stone. He had a high rasping voice that carried to the far corners of the flower patch.

"Fellow noxious insect eaters . . . " he began. All heads turned. This was something new.

"Fellow noxious insect eaters. We all know unfairness
only too well. We keep the noxious insects in check and
so the pets are not troubled by mosquitoes."

Everyone cheered. Shrew seemed to grow larger at

the sound, and his voice grew deeper and stronger to rise over the cheers. "Our very names are insults." He pointed at each in turn, "Snake in the grass. Lowdown Skunk. Bats in the belfry. Toad. Spider. Shrew. These are not pet names."

An uproar broke out. The flowers swayed. Voices were raised over the confusion to shout for order, and, after a bit, it did get quieter. Shrew shouted, "But now it seems that things are to be arranged so that it rains only on us and not on them. Something must be done."

Snake asked, "Well, whose fault is that?"

Shrew snapped back amid more cheers, "I *know* whose fault it is. Didn't you hear that conversation on the terrace today? While we were being drenched, a voice from nowhere says sweetly, 'Rain ending tonight. Fair and warmer tomorrow.' That proves how that man controls the weather."

One spider who had wintered in the house was explaining TV and another was describing the warmth when Toad spoke up: "Isn't everything really up to the man on the terrace? I mean I have written a little poem that I think says it all." Without waiting he began to chant in a low monotone that claimed everyone's attention:

While we stumble in darkest night
He reads a book in his private light.
While rain pours down on us alone
His pets are sunning dry as bone.
He empties the pool at his own sweet will
And just as calmly lets it fill.
He stays warm in winter's snows
And why he does things—no one knows.

There was an astonished silence after Toad's recital. At last Shrew said, "Toad's right. It's the man in the house who makes things happen." He added bitterly, "And he favors the pets."

Shouts came from all sides.

"The man doesn't know that we are the ones who hold down the insects."

"Yes. All the pets do is sit around."

"Let's all go see him."

"No, send a committee."

"Send Shrew."

"Hooray for Shrew."

Shrew waved for silence. "We must not be rushed into careless action. We need a plan. We need organization."

Skunk said happily, "I move we elect a president, vice-president, secretary and treasurer."

Bat said, "Don't forget the minutes," and flew away. Heads nodded in the silence that followed. Yes, that was it. An organization to take care of everything. Greatly relieved at having settled their problem, they began to drift away into the night. It was bedtime for the babies. The moles went underground, and soon only Toad, Snake, Father Skunk and some mantises and spiders remained around Shrew. Bat, tirelessly snapping up flying insects overhead, let a gentle rain of gossamer wings and beetle shells fall on the heads of the little group.

Shrew said, "I guess we are it."

Snake asked, "What are we supposed to do?" and they all looked at Shrew.

"Well, first it must rain fairly on everyone alike. Then

we want the right to use the pool without danger of attack."

Snake said, "Yes, that is what we want. But what are we going to do?"

Skunk wanted to draw up rules and elect officers. Bat, a voice from the sky, said, "Put it in the paper." No one paid any attention; Bat was known to be light minded. Toad suggested that they write letters to the man. "He couldn't ignore us all," said Toad. Then a spider said that it was getting late and everyone began to shuffle around getting ready to go. "Wait," said Shrew. "I have an idea. Why not really put things in the paper? The man sits by the pool for hours at a time reading newspapers and watching his pets. Suppose he were to read that his pets were good for nothing but carrying disease, or climbing trees and having to be rescued by firemen. Suppose he then read that his garden was full of unseen friends who kept noxious insects from biting him and from destroying his flowers. How would he feel then?"

Everyone stopped shuffling and waited for Shrew to go on. He didn't. Bat skimmed down and said, "It is news when man bites dog. It is also news when dog bites man." They all waved him away.

"Don't interrupt."

"This is serious."

They stood in silent thought a little longer. At last Skunk suggested that they arrange a time and place for the next meeting.

"Wait," said Shrew. "Suppose we wrote out news stories and took them to town to the editor of the newspaper, and suppose they were interesting stories. Why wouldn't they get printed?"

"I'll carry the mail," sang Bat from the stars.

"Yes. Let Bat deliver the stories. He can do it."

"But can he be trusted?"

"Who else is there?"

"It's not much of a plan," said Toad with a sniff.

"It's the best we've got," said Shrew. "We have to take some action. We will write stories about how much good we do and about what nuisances the pets are. Bat, you get them to the newspaper editor's desk. When our stories are printed the man will know who his true friends are. Why should he favor the pets? He will then make the rain fall fairly; he might even feed us and allow us to use the pool in peace."

"Well," said Toad, "we have nothing to lose."

Skunk felt quite cheered by the plan. "We should have a real organization with a name. How about calling ourselves the Noxious Insect Eaters Management Associates? The initials spell out N–I–E–M–A."

Snake said gently, "Shouldn't we refer to ourselves rather as Eaters of Noxious Insects? To avoid confusion?"

Skunk disagreed. He liked NIEMA. But when Snake suggested that the name could be Eaters of Noxious Insects General Management Associates, or E–N–I–G–M–A, Skunk was appeased and graciously agreed.

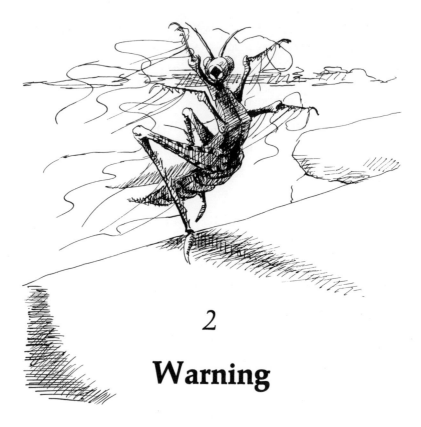

2

Warning

ENIGMA GOT VERY BUSY. Skunk salvaged some clean white paper from the garbage dump. Toad produced some gay quill pens made from the tail feathers of a molting blue jay. Two spiders brought in a frightened grasshopper tightly bound with spider's silk. He was to be the ink supply; when pressed he would bring up a blob of brown liquid which made a good clear ink.

Everyone assembled in the flower-patch headquarters.

Shrew was dictating: "A shrew consumes his weight in harmful insects every three hours."

Toad, who was writing, said, "We've got that one."

"How many do we have altogether?"

"Ninety-five."

Toad read back: "The common toad is one of the gardener's best friends. He eats Japanese beetles. The snake eats slugs and harmful grubs. A skunk is . . ."

Shrew interrupted. "Have you got the statistics on the pets?"

Toad shuffled through the pile of papers. "Last year, firemen answered 7,489 alarms to rescue cats from trees, chimneys and other high places. Parrots carry psittacosis, or parrot fever. Their import is carefully regulated. Rabies claimed x victims last year, mostly children. Rabies is carried by dogs."

"What do you mean x?"

"I haven't been able to find the exact number."

"Say over a thousand."

Snake interrupted. "May I suggest that our stories might have more effect if we all stopped eating noxious insects while they were being published? If the man has to slap mosquitoes while reading the paper and finds his flowers eaten by Japanese beetles he may be more likely to pay attention."

Bat said, "Hooray."

Skunk wanted to know what was he supposed to eat, and Toad looked unhappy. Snake said, "Eat worms. The garden is full of them."

All ENIGMA members liked worms except Bat, who didn't count. He could manage on harmless moths.

Bat said from underneath an overhead branch, "First ninety-five articles and then a Diet of Worms," and choked with laughter. The members of ENIGMA looked at each other and shook their heads.

Shrew glared at Bat. "We are counting on you. If these stories are not delivered to the right desk the whole plan fails."

Bat vanished before Shrew finished speaking. Shrew turned to Snake and said, "Could you take them and crawl through a crack or something?"

Snake shook his head. "Bat is all right," he said, and added silently, "I hope."

Bat reappeared, picked up Toad's neat pile of papers and tossed them into the air. He cleverly caught them in a little pouch he had under his tail and asked, "Should I nail these to the door?"

Shrew lost his temper. "You are to fly through the ventilator of the newspaper office and put them in the basket marked *Copy* on the editor's desk. If anything goes wrong you will be blamed and executed for treason. You hear me?" Bat had gone. "I don't trust anything that flies," muttered Shrew.

There was now nothing to do. After all the hope and activity it was hard to just sit still. Toad and Snake started a complicated word game.

"I'm thinking of H."

"Hairy?"

"You're very cold."

No one else took part. Shrew hunted crickets in the shadows while Skunk dug around the roots of the flowers. One of the mantises opened its claws and slid up to the captive grasshopper.

"Not yet," said Skunk. "We may need him." The grasshopper rolled his eyes.

THE NEXT MORNING, over a cup of coffee, the editor looked through a pile of papers on his desk. "Fascinating," he murmured. "Hey, did you know that a mole eats his weight in harmful insects every twenty-four hours?" He called the office boy over. "Did you write these?" he asked.

The boy tried to read the right answer in the editor's face. He couldn't, so he kicked at the floor and blushed. "Good job!" said the editor. "Just what we need. Every-

one wants to read about the wonders of Nature. I have an inch at the bottom of column three on page two that's just right for moles, and this one will fill the space over the tire ad on page eight." The editor grew busy with his red pencil and the boy tiptoed away.

"What was all that about?" he asked the mail clerk.

"Some nut." The mail clerk shrugged.

ENIGMA HAD SCATTERED and gone into hiding for the day, each creature in its separate hole. In a shady thicket, Skunk was tending the splendid tail that soared over his black back in a silver spray. He was very vain and spent hours seeing that each hair fell just right. Bat had returned from his errand to the high hollow tree that he shared with his relatives. He looked out of a tiny knothole and hummed *Stouthearted Men* a few times and then told his relatives all about ENIGMA.

"What will you do now?" one wanted to know.

"Nothing," said Bat. "We have started things moving. Now we can only wait and see." He continued to hum *Stouthearted Men* and occasionally chuckled softly through the tiny knothole.

The sun climbed higher, and the temperature with it. A heat haze hung in silence that was only deepened by

the sad far-off moan of a mourning dove. The captive grasshopper, left unguarded in the flower patch, worked without hope at his bonds. He wriggled on hour after hour. Nothing else moved.

THE PETS LAY quietly panting in the shade and watched the reflections in the still pool shimmer through the heat waves. They didn't have enough energy to quarrel.

They usually spent the greater part of their day being scientifically trained by Dr. Ordley. The doctor was very encouraged at the moment by Dog and Cat who never left the terrace and never attacked the hamsters. Of course, they never played either, and always seemed irritable. The doctor felt that perhaps they were working too hard learning to be peaceable, so they were resting while he concentrated on Duck.

Duck felt it her duty to patrol the pool, and besides she enjoyed admiring her reflection in the still water between the lily pads. As the doctor watched Duck on patrol he realized he would need his best equipment to train her to keep out of the pool.

He chose the newest thing from the Olympian Scientific Equipment Corporation—their Thunderbolt Stunner. The Stunner was a black box covered with dials

and switches that could send an electric charge through
the water to a special ring fastened around Duck's ankle.
The doctor adjusted the voltage dial to low—just enough
for a nasty jolt. He waited and watched. When Duck
went into the pool he pressed a red button on the Stunner.

Duck learned quickly. Squawking didn't help—

neither did diving, wing flapping or rapid swimming, either straight or in circles. The only way to stop the shocks in her ankle, she decided, was to get out of the pool.

She joined the pets in the shade to brood about secret evil forces while the others thought how much prettier the pool reflections were at night when the house lights sparkled in the black water. The doctor felt it was time to note the progress in Duck's training, so he retired to his cool shady laboratory and began writing in his notebook. He stretched out on a leather sofa for greater comfort while he worked. He did not reappear.

The perfect peace was suddenly broken by shrill cries from the garden below. All heads lifted and eyes turned to the steps. The cries continued and presently an exhausted grasshopper, trailing ropes of gray spider silk, heaved up and stumbled in collapse on the terrace.

"Beware ENIGMA!" he gasped out, and fainted dead away.

3
CRUMB

"There I was," said the grasshopper, "tied hand and foot in their secret headquarters in the flower patch. This mantis came stealing toward me, clicking his horrible claws. Cold perspiration burst out on my forehead. There was no escape! I could feel his jaws closing on me when the skunk, a well-known grasshopper eater, decided to save me for himself and told the mantis that

I would be *useful later*. I thanked the merciful providence that watches over grasshoppers."

The grasshopper, who, much recovered, had become the pet's pet, was reclining in the shade two days later while he retold his fearful adventures for the third time.

The pets burst into delighted applause. He was better than TV.

"What happened next?" cried a hamster.

"Then they all plotted some more about their secret society and how, when you were all killed, ENIGMA would take over."

"How were we going to be killed?"

"Your master would do it after he read the newspaper stories that they had planted."

The dog growled. "I have never heard such nonsense in my life. To think that a newspaper would print stories by a scruffy little bunch of wild animals. Why, it's ridiculous."

"Just let them come up here," said the cat, stretching out her front claws. "I'd love it."

The duck said solemnly, "I can't think what's gotten into them. We belong up here and they belong down there. It has always been that way. Somebody must be stirring them up."

The dog asked, "Have you seen anything strange hanging around?"

The grasshopper thought a bit and said that one of the spiders that grabbed him had been hanging from a leaf.

"No, not that kind of hanging. Something strange."

The grasshopper thought that a spider seen close up was pretty strange, but he kept the thought to himself. "There was this horrible bat with long teeth and red eyes," he said.

"A vampire!" cried the duck. "I knew it. I could feel something like that going on."

"This is more serious than I thought," said the dog. "What else did they say?"

"Well, they said that they would stop eating noxious insects so that the garden would be ruined."

"That's the vampire's work!" screamed the duck. "Heaven only knows what they will be eating as long as that vampire has them in his power. Preserve us all!"

The dog looked grim. His jaw set and his tail stuck out straight. "Everybody keep calm. I think that we had better have a look at the papers. Cat?"

The cat said, "I'm sure you can still read them," and went to her box and scratched out the torn bits of newspaper. They all gathered around.

It was quite a jigsaw puzzle to put the scraps together,

but they managed it. The hamsters were good at fitting the pieces so that the words matched.

"Boy," said a hamster, "look at that headline, 'No Relief In Sight From Record Heat.'"

Another one got interested in the comics.

"Let's not forget what we are here for," said the dog.

"Look!" screeched the duck. "'Rabies claimed over a thousand victims last year, mostly children. Rabies is carried by dogs.' Look! Right over that tire ad."

"And another! 'The toad is the gardener's friend. . . .' Another vampire story!"

"Here's another one at the bottom of page two. 'A mole eats his weight in harmful insects every twenty-four hours.'"

"Let me see that."

"It's a vampire plot."

"Don't take away my paper. I'm reading."

A scuffle started over the scraps. The cat said it was her paper anyway. The dog was so hot and angry that he began to growl. The duck pushed in front of him and he snapped at her. She screamed "Rabies!" The dog, furious, growled "Vampire!" and leaped at her. The grasshopper, forgotten, was accidentally kicked into the pool.

He swam across the pool to safety. From the other side he looked back at the knot of struggling pets shouting in the hot sunshine. "Mad, all mad," he said, and disappeared into the tall grass.

A harsh voice rose over the babble on the terrace. "Vampires? Who said vampires? I know all about vampires." The voice came from the parrot in the shade.

These were the first words she had ever addressed to the pets. They were so astonished that they forgot their quarrel. Until that moment she had only spoken to humans and then only to ask for a cracker, whistle and swear. Since she always got her cracker, the pets thought that she was probably very wise. She was certainly old.

"I can tell you a thing or two about vampires," she continued. "Vampires can steal up on you at night through the thickest jungle and get you while you are peacefully asleep in a palm tree. That's what vampires are like."

"Jungle?" asked Cat.

"Palm tree?" asked Duck.

"Yes, jungle. There is a lot more to life than just swimming and playing on this nice cool patio while the doctor feeds and educates you."

"Cool!" panted Cat.

28

"Yes, cool. In the big real world there is a fiercer sun in a hotter sky than any you know in your little corner. Now that the vampires have arrived here maybe real life will start at last."

"Real life? What's real life?" asked Lamb.

"Real life is harsh and full of evil things that are out to get you. It's dog eat dog."

Dog objected. "I am a dog in real life. I wouldn't think of eating dog. I eat enriched soybean paste only."

Parrot sneered at him. "That is because you are a good dog." She shrieked at him suddenly, "Aren't you?"

Dog nodded nervously. "I am a good dog."

Parrot went on, "And the reason you are a good dog is . . . ?"

Dog looked bewildered. "Well, there are lots of reasons," he said. "For instance, I'm loyal."

Parrot said, "Isn't the main reason that you are obedient?"

Dog nodded eagerly. "Yes. Yes, that's it. I'm obedient."

Parrot did a fair imitation of the doctor's voice: *"Then Come Here."*

Dog trotted up to her.

"Sit." He sat.

"*Roll Over.*" He rolled. It was his best trick and he was proud of it. Dog got up wagging his tail and looked pleased.

Parrot said, "You are a good dog. See to it that you remain one. Now sit." Dog sat.

"Now listen," Parrot continued. "Soft times are over. Vampires are here, and with them come the toads, snakes and spiders. How would you like this pleasant place, our place, overrun by skunks? That's just what they are plotting unless we take action. You've seen the evidence. You have been warned."

There was a low mutter at this from the pets. Lamb put his ears back and lowered his head. "What should we do?" asked Dog.

"Organize yourselves for defense. Remember, a stitch in time saves nine. A word to the wise is sufficient."

The pets all began to talk at once.

"What did she say?"

"What does it mean?"

"What word?"

From his position under the parrot's perch, Dog barked, "Quiet! You heard the word. We must have an organization." He looked fiercely at the murmuring pets. The hamsters became worried.

The duck perked up. She loved organizations. "We must choose officers and a nice name. Let's call ourselves . . . Let's see . . ." and she closed her eyes.

Parrot's rough voice broke in, "Your name will be the Committee to Restore Universal Moral Balance. Dog will be in charge and you will all take your orders from me."

Duck opened her eyes. "Committee to Restore Universal Moral Balance. C–R–U–M–B. Very nice. We will call ourselves Crumbs."

"Call yourselves anything you like." Parrot's fiery eye glared down at them from its white circle. "But get it through your heads that this is an emergency. Vampires are after us. They must be destroyed."

Cat objected. "We are peaceful pets. We never destroy anything."

Parrot looked at her in amazement. "Do you call yourself a cat? Don't you know anything about being a real cat? Real cats steal along the highest branches. Then they crouch and slink and leap and even the swiftest monkey isn't safe."

Cat lashed her tail. Parrot watched her. "Cat! Look at the soft furry hamsters! Look at your claws! Can't you see what they're for?"

Cat was overcome by Parrot's insight. A green glare seemed to fill her head and she heard Parrot say faintly, as through a roar of wind, "Hold it! Save it for the vampires!" The words stopped her just in time. The terrified hamsters whipped out a white handkerchief and held it out to her.

"And Dog! You are swift so that you can catch a fleeing animal and shake it in those strong jaws." Dog growled. Parrot was a wizard. She knew Dog's secret dreams. "Now catch and shake the vampires! If you don't, you will have a pool full of snakes." Duck quacked angrily.

Parrot's speech had a tremendous effect on the pets. Everything was clear! They would defend their patio!

Parrot went on, "I have traveled and seen the world. I tell you that no one is ever safe from vampires. There is only one defense. Kill them! Kill them! Kill them!" Parrot stamped from side to side on her perch in a frenzy, shrieking, her chain rattling, and seeds scattering beneath her. The pets crouched in a scared silence. A hamster whispered, "What did she say?" There was no answer.

At last the dog bounded up. "We will attack tonight! We will defend the patio!" A perfect riot of cheers followed. The hamsters went wild with joy and relief that they were not the ones to be attacked and started to dance. Dr. Ordley came out to see what the noise was about. "I wonder where they get the energy to play in this heat," he said yawning, as he returned to his cool leather sofa.

CRUMB SPENT the rest of the afternoon making plans. "Grasshopper says their headquarters is in the flower patch. They will all be there."

"We've got them against the wall. It is a natural trap."

"There'll be no way out."

It was decided that after dark they would form a half circle around the flower patch with Dog in the center

34

and Cat and Lamb on each end. Duck and the hamsters would fill in the spaces in the rear. When they were in position Dog would give the signal to charge and they would close in and wipe out the enemy.

"What about the vampire bat?" Duck wanted to know.

"You leave that bat to me," said Parrot, and she snapped her heavy gray beak.

4

Eve of Battle

CRUMB WAITED FOR DARKNESS. The heat continued—there was still no wind and not a leaf moved. As it grew darker there was distant heat lightning and low thunder. When the last light faded Cat was sent to scout the flower patch. She was under strict orders not to be seen.

While she was gone, Dog, now Colonel Dog by the parrot's order, called the roll.

"Private Hamster, G."

"Here."

"Private Hamster, T."

"Here."

"Private Hamster, Y."

"Here."

"Corporal Duck."

"Here, sir!"

They had all tied leaves around their heads for camouflage. Corporal Duck had included some rosebuds in her headdress. No detail had been overlooked. . . . They were ready.

It grew pitch dark. A little light came from the house, but the fireflies still dazzled the eye. Some of the hamsters had been posted as sentries to guard against . . . what? No one asked. They were looking about nervously. The lamb, who had heard somewhere that an old soldier always sleeps when not in action, was curled in a woolly ball. Colonel Dog went among the troops keeping up morale. "Hiya fella," he said to a hamster, who smiled back eagerly. "Everything O.K.?"

"Oh, yes, sir!" said the hamster. "Everything is all gung ho, sir."

"Good show," answered Colonel Dog.

"Lance Corporal Lamb?"

"Sir?"

"Were you asleep?"

"Yes, sir."

"Good show." Colonel Dog thought to himself that war brought out the best qualities in troops. Who would have expected Lamb to be so cool at such a tense moment? He considered giving Lamb a medal for showing exceptional bravery before battle. Good old Lamb! All his usual disgust and annoyance with Lamb was forgotten. They were comrades in arms.

One of the sentries in the dark suddenly called in a trembling voice, "Halt. Who is there?" Colonel Dog was on him in an instant.

"Get that sentry's name! Hamster, stand to attention! Stop that shaking. Don't you know the proper way to give a challenge? Do you think you are answering a telephone? You say, 'Halt. Who goes there? Friend or foe?'" He then looked out into the darkness and said, "Is anyone there?"

Captain Cat came up the terrace steps. "They are in the flower patch," she said.

Colonel Dog called his officers for a last briefing. "You all know your positions. Keep your eyes on me and hold

those lines straight. Don't get ahead or fall behind. Keep a low silhouette. When I bark three times, charge. Good luck."

"Will you get a move on!" the parrot said hoarsely from her perch. She was twisting her chain in her powerful beak. A link snapped.

The CRUMB army stole out in good formation. They headed for the flower patch at the far end of the garden. Each pet kept his head down and crawled in perfect time.

Bat watched them silently from the night sky.

AT ENIGMA HEADQUARTERS the mood was gloomy. "How do you know they were not printed?" Snake wanted to know.

Toad said, "Does it seem likely to you that they were? We must have been crazy. Why, the chances are a hundred to one against it."

Shrew said, "I'll bet that Bat never even delivered them. He's afraid to face us. Just wait till I get my paws on him."

"Skunk will bring the papers as soon as they get thrown out. That may take another few days," Snake said. "We won't really know till then, so cheer up. We're not beaten. There is still our no-noxious-insect-eating policy."

"Which is wearing me to a frazzle."

"And which can't do any good anyway because no one up there even knows that we are doing it—or not doing it."

"If we could somehow get in touch with them to let them know, then maybe they would be frightened."

"That's impossible. We have no contact with them."

Bat appeared and hung head down from a tall hollyhock. "Hey, wake up down there. There's a war on."

"Very funny," said Shrew. "Where have you been? Did you by chance remember to deliver those papers we worked on so hard? Hey?"

"Of course I did. But now forget the papers. I came to warn you. You are being attacked."

"Forget the papers!" screamed Shrew. "I'll kill you."

Bat said very slowly and distinctly, "At this moment the pets are creeping up on you. They have you surrounded. They mean business."

Shrew shouted, "What are you talking about? The pets? In the garden? In the dark? You're crazy. What happened to those papers?"

Bat interrupted, "Where is Skunk?"

Shrew ignored this and, gnashing his teeth, cried, "Did you or didn't you deliver those papers? Answer me!"

"Oh God," said Bat and flew off.

CRUMB CREPT CLOSER. Colonel Dog risked raising his head for a look. Yes—there was Lamb, pale in the darkness, at his proper post anchoring the corner of the line. A good comrade in a fight—a cool reliable ally. And Captain Cat, deadly and fierce—Colonel Dog could see her green eyes shining at the other end of the line. Corporal Duck's rosebuds were waving gently in the rear at the head of the support troops. Everything was ready. And yet he hesitated before giving the signal. No one knew what could happen in a battle. Peace was sweet and he wished to enjoy one more quiet moment with his loyal troops before casting them all into the flames of war. At last he could wait no longer. They were all poised. Colonel Dog barked three times.

SHREW WAS STILL GNASHING his teeth after Bat flew off. He turned to ENIGMA. "He must be tried for treason. There are enough of us here to make up a court. I vote that he is guilty."

Snake thought that Bat should have an opportunity to defend himself.

"You were always soft on bats."

"What is that supposed to mean?" said Snake, and he wound himself into a dark coil in front of Shrew.

Shrew bristled. "Just what it sounds like."

Toad wailed, "Oh, please don't fight. I can't stand fighting."

Then they heard a dog bark three times, right in their ears.

5

Battle

THE SURPRISE WAS COMPLETE. ENIGMA had its back to the wall. CRUMB was between them and the freedom of the garden. Dog thrust his head, white teeth shining, right at Shrew. Cat slashed out at Snake who was still coiled in fighting stance.

"Surrender!" said Colonel Dog.

"Terms?" cried Shrew.

"Paws over your head and come out one at a time."

Toad's white throat, shaking in extreme agitation, could be seen shining in the darkness. Suddenly he screamed and ran. He dashed right at Lance Corporal Lamb in a panic and kicked him in the shin while trying to get through. Lamb nervously leaped to avoid the kick and came down on Toad, who kicked him again. Feeling a soft squirming something under his hoof, and neither knowing what it was nor liking it, Lance Corporal Lamb also panicked and ran off bleating and shaking his hoof. Shrew saw the hole in the CRUMB battle line and, shouting "This way, ENIGMA!" dashed through it with Snake and a rush of mantises and spiders at his heels. Before Colonel Dog could re-group his forces, ENIGMA had streamed out into the second line of defense.

Shrew ran into Private Hamster, G. who cried, "Halt. Who goes there? Friend or foe?" Shrew bit him severely on the cheek, which started to swell.

Fighting scattered through the dark garden. Dog was making a great uproar dashing about and not managing to find the enemy. The hamsters were clustered around Private Hamster, G., who was down. The duck, with spread wings, slowly circled Toad who was crying out that he was a poet, not a soldier. In the center of the garden, Cat stalked Shrew who, seeing no escape, faced her bravely.

Cat feinted at Shrew with a lightning stroke that just nicked the top of his head. Shrew snapped back at the paw, too late. Cat loved this kind of play and was prepared to toy with Shrew indefinitely, forgetting the rest of the battle.

"Why did you attack us?" gasped Shrew.

"Why did you put all those lies in the paper about cats being rescued out of tall trees by firemen?" and another quick stroke rolled Shrew over. He got up bleeding over one eye. So! Good old Bat! He had come through after all. Shrew tried a charge. His cause was hopeless but he was determined to go down fighting.

Cat had heard that a shrew's bite is painful and carries poison. Shrews also send out a strong musky scent when angry. So Cat danced lightly aside.

"Charge, ENIGMA!" cried Shrew.

"Charge, CRUMB!" answered Colonel Dog and rushed to the cry.

Shrew's brave shout in the dark now gave the battle a new center. Snake and the mantises and spiders converged on the cry shouting, "ENIGMA, ENIGMA!"

They arrived simultaneously with Colonel Dog, who
bellowed, "CRUMB, CRUMB!" and began to snap at
the mantises who snapped back. Snake, seeing how
things stood with Shrew, struck and bit the cat's ear. Cat
whirled. Snake was whipped violently around, and
Shrew dodged.

"Good old Snake saved my life!" thought Shrew and pulled the cat's tail.

Cat whirled back and Snake let go of Cat's ear and escaped. "Good old Shrew saved my life!" thought Snake.

Colonel Dog and Captain Cat were strong fighters, so even though ENIGMA had scored some early victories, Shrew called for a general retreat. That was easier said than done.

Dog was leaping and biting at mantises and spiders who had nipped him painfully in several tender places. Duck left Toad and ran to help Dog. She grabbed a spider, which made the others more careful. Shrew tried to retreat from Captain Cat who was again stalking him. Dog, given some rest by the spiders, began to bark at Snake. The tables were turning.

Just as things started to look black for ENIGMA, a faint call came from the dark sky. *Rat-ti ta-ti-ta-ti ta-ti-taah*. Bat was overhead imitating, in his high clear voice, the cavalry charge bugle call. ENIGMA cheered the new arrival as he darted into Cat's face and away. Only Toad, who was retreating successfully, saw what followed Bat. "Oh my goodness," Toad gasped, and he took a deep breath.

Father on the right, Mother on the left, and the four babies in between, the entire Skunk family came charging into the battle and laid down an awful barrage. Father's salvos scored direct hits on Colonel Dog who somersaulted backwards and began yelping and rubbing his face in the grass. Captain Cat leaped high in the air to escape, but Mother Skunk got her coming down. Cat yowled and streaked for the nearest tree. The babies, giggling with joy, sprayed friend and foe alike with their fearful scent. It was every warrior for himself as they all ran for safety.

In a moment the reeking, steaming garden, so recently a fierce battlefield, was an empty desert. A terrible fog floated over the silence.

The Skunks, tails high, trotted back to their hunting in the field where Bat had found them. Bat himself, weak from laughter, was headed for a perch in a tree to rest. "Stouthearted men," he gasped, and he staggered about the sky as another fit of laughter seized him. He noted Cat's unhappy form balled up in the top branches of a tall oak tree and changed direction for a dense pine. His eyes full of tears, he barely reached a safe branch.

A cruel claw grabbed him about the middle. Bat looked up into an insane eye rolling in a white circle.

"Got you!" said Parrot.

6

Victory

IN THE DAWN after the battle both sides counted their losses and claimed victory. The choking fog still hung over the windless garden. Japanese beetles had eaten all the flowers. Slugs had chewed the foliage. There was a low humming in the heavy air.

The parrot had ordered a memorial service for the fallen. Captain Cat was missing and presumed dead.

No one had seen her after the attack. There had been that scream, and then silence. Lamb thought that the skunks had carried her off, but wasn't sure. Private Hamster, G. was severely wounded. His head had swollen so that his eyes were shut and he was running a fever. They all stood quietly to attention while Duck played Taps on a paper and comb. As the last notes faded, the hamsters wept openly and Colonel Dog set his teeth as he stared at the blighted garden through a film of tears.

"Goodbye, Captain Cat. May you rest in peace, wherever you are."

After a moment of reverent silence, the parrot broke in harshly, "We have won. The ENIGMA plot is over. I have captured their leader." She flew dramatically to the pine tree and returned with poor Bat, wrapped in her broken chain, clutched in her claws.

At the sight of Bat, the pets released their breaths in a long-drawn "Oooh." Parrot said, "We must question the prisoner. Your name?"

"Bat."

"A likely story. I suggest your name is Count Dracula, and that you are a Transylvanian vampire."

"If you say so."

The parrot turned to the listening pets. "Take note that he admits he is a vampire."

The pets crowded together in equal fear of the parrot's fierce eye and the terrible bat.

"Why did you lead the insect eaters against us?"

"I didn't lead them."

"Oh no?"

"I just flew errands and delivered messages. You might say that I was their errand bat."

"The picture of innocence. I suggest that you turned

the creatures into vampires so that they stopped eating their natural wholesome insect foods," said Parrot. "Just look at the uneaten insects overrunning that garden and try to deny it. Then you led the skunk charge. I saw you do that myself. Now do you deny that you were the leader?"

"Well, yes, in a way I guess I did do that last bit."

Parrot turned to the pets. "No matter how he squirms and tries to mislead us, the truth is so clear that he cannot deny it."

"Vampire, vampire. He admits it," they shouted.

"We never attacked you. You started the fighting. I only brought in the skunks to stop it."

The dog came forward and growled, "You put those lies about us in the paper in order to turn our master

54

against us. Then you planned to kill us and take over our patio. You attacked us. We may only be peaceful pets but we will defend our lives. You can't fool us as if we were your insect eaters, you blood drinker."

"Very good, Colonel Dog," said Parrot and Dog saluted and stepped back into the ranks. Parrot then held up the end of her chain. "What shall we do with the vampire?"

"Hang the vampire!" cried the pets in a chorus.

Skunk meanwhile was apologizing to ENIGMA. "I'm sorry. It was the children. My wife and I were very careful how we aimed, but you know how children are." The smell in the garden was terrible.

Shrew gasped, "We all thank you for saving our lives. I also want to thank Snake for saving me from that cat."

Snake raised his head from a mole hole where the air was a bit better. "You saved my life, too."

"Toad saved us all by breaking their line."

"The spiders and mantises saved us by keeping that dog so busy."

"Bat saved us by bringing the Skunks."

"Bat tried to warn us."

"Bat got our stories printed in the newspaper."

"Where is Bat?"

No one knew. "We must find Bat. Tell him that he can come out in daylight now. We won our victory."

Swift spider scouts scattered to look for Bat. Some went to his hollow tree. Others, knowing that the air would be better on the terrace, went there. "Look out for that duck," they warned each other.

The terrace group was back in a short time. "Bat is in chains up there. The pets are going to hang him."

This report set off furious activity. Shrew cried fiercely, "We beat them in the garden, we will beat them on the patio and in the pool."

Snake said, "We must have a plan of rescue."

They quickly decided to form a flying wedge and attack the terrace. Skunk would lead and the rest would follow. If there was any resistance, Skunk would fire.

"Charge!" they shouted and, forming up in the long early morning shadow cast by Skunk's raised tail, they raced for the terrace stairs.

ON THE TERRACE, Parrot looped her chain around Bat's neck. "Have you any last words?"

"Would they do any good?" Bat wanted to know.

"None at all."

"Then here goes nothing." Bat turned to the pets. "This bird is crazy. I am not a vampire. There is no such place as Transylvania."

"Oh, ho, but you are wrong there," said a hamster. "I've seen it on TV and it is full of bats."

"Well, if it is on the TV maybe it is so, but I have never been there. I was born in the garden, as were all the rest of us. We don't watch TV and we don't live in a warm house in the winter. Neither can we play in the sun nor swim in the pool. We do keep the garden free of harmful insects, though. We do this at night while you sleep."

"Finished?" asked the parrot.

"One minute more. Yes, there was a plot. But we only plotted to come out in the daylight without being pounced on. We only plotted to be able to use the pool in hot weather."

"Lies!" cried the dog. "We pets never pounce on anything."

Duck shuddered. "Snakes and toads in the pool!"

The hamsters said, "Spiders all over the patio!"

"Finished now?" asked Parrot, pushing Bat off the perch. Bat fell with a snap to the end of the chain and swung to and fro. The pets all cheered.

Skunk appeared, out of breath, at the top of the steps. "Where's Bat?" he said.

"Surrender!" cried Shrew right behind him.

The pets turned in dead silence and, at the sight of Skunk, cowered together.

"Fight!" screamed Parrot at the huddled pets. "Charge!" and she zoomed down at Skunk.

Parrot, who had been high in a tree during the battle, didn't know what a skunk was like at close range. Now she found out. Skunk turned, tail high over his back, and fired one short burst which hit Parrot squarely on the breast. Squawking terribly, her eyes blinded by tears, green feathers flying in a cloud, Parrot clawed and flew

end over end up to the peak of the roof where she perched in the morning sunshine and used such language as had never been heard before. Both groups of animals drew a little closer together and cringed in horror at the awful things Parrot was saying. Snake slid into the pool, saying that he wanted a bath. It was while he was enjoying his first swim there that he saw Bat.

Snake's cry drew everyone's attention to him. Following his horrified stare, ENIGMA discovered Bat, now slowly rotating, at the end of the chain.

Shrew undid the chain. Bat dropped to the terrace stones with a soft plop and lay very still.

7

And After

Dr. Ordley, D.V.M., began each day by tending his animals; only after he had done so would he have breakfast.

On the morning after the battle of the garden he looked out of his window, and saw a snake in the pool. Looking farther, he saw a skunk licking the dog's dish, a small dark shrew darting about, and a toad. He got out his notebook and wrote excitedly: "This morning a whole new stage of my experiment began. The wild things came up on the terrace. Not one stray accidental animal, but a number of different kinds. This shows what love can do. They have found out that they are safe here. They have found out that neither the dog nor the cat will attack them. How? Is there an odor of love?" He saw his garden as a peaceable kingdom in which the cat would lie down with the mouse. He went outside to study some more.

The first thing he noticed was that something must have alarmed the skunk. What a powerful skunk that was, thought the doctor, holding a handkerchief to his nose. He noted the absence of Cat, and Parrot's empty perch. "No wonder they've gone. They will be back when it clears," he said through the handkerchief.

ENIGMA watched the doctor tensely to see what he would do. This was the moment. Skunk was ready.

The doctor saw Bat at his feet and picked him up very gently, examined him carefully, and wrapped him in his handkerchief. Then poor Private Hamster, G., his head still decorated with leaves and nearly double its size, caught his eye. The doctor held the unconscious animal in his hand while he pondered the questions

raised by that swollen and decorated head. He found no
ready answers so he wrapped the hamster in the handkerchief beside Bat and very carefully took them into
the house.

He then brought out breakfast for both sets of ani-
mals. The pets received their usual scientific diet, but
Skunk got a dish of hamburger and hard-boiled egg.
The doctor produced some ant eggs and meal worms
from his stores that exactly suited Snake, Toad and
Shrew.

The parrot on the roof bitterly watched the doctor
tending the wild things. A great sadness filled her. Her
pleasant life of summer on the patio and winter by the

television set was over. She would not live with snakes, toads, skunks and vampire bats. Dogs and cats were bad enough.

Her attempt to defend them all against invasion had failed—not because they were defeated; they weren't. True, she hadn't reckoned with Skunk, but she could deal with that. What she could not deal with was the doctor's betrayal. He had welcomed *them* in! There was nothing left here. Parrot thought wistfully of the wide green jungle where she had been born. There a noxious insect was a noxious insect and a snake was a snake, not like that miserable noodle down by the pool. She had seen snakes forty feet long, shiny beetles nearly as big as footballs, and fierce spotted cats who loved to eat parrots. There, in the hot sun, by the great slow brown jungle rivers, was a life that she could understand. This soft existence on the patio suddenly seemed dull and meaningless. She had had enough of being chained to a perch; she would go home. She flew off the roof and headed south to the Amazon.

No one noticed Parrot's departure. They were all staring at each other. The insect eaters were clustered around Skunk, whose raised white tail floated over them like a flag of truce.

"Get off our patio!" growled Dog.

"We are here to stay!" answered Shrew.

Dog glared. "If you would fight fair, like gentlemen, we'd soon see how long you'd stay. But here you are, for the time being, due to trickery and poison gas."

Shrew said, "I suppose your weapons are fair and ours aren't because we beat you. Do you think hanging prisoners is a gentleman's trick?"

"He was a vampire. You are all vampires."

Shrew did not know what a vampire was, but the spider who had spent the winter in the house and had watched TV explained. Shrew got angry. "Any more insults and off the terrace you go. From now on you will only speak when spoken to and will keep off our side of the terrace. You may use the pool and food dishes only when we are not using them. We will give you further orders when we are ready. You hear me?"

Dog was stunned. This was the meaning of defeat. It was too much to bear, and on his own patio, too. He looked helplessly at Duck who looked at Lamb who looked away and tried to butt the hamsters. The hamsters snapped back at him and Lamb retreated. Dog, who was still smarting from spider bites, wondered whether the hamsters would attack him next. He sud-

denly thought of Parrot. Parrot would know what to do.

"Where is Parrot?" he asked. All the pets looked up at the roof anxiously. "Parrot, Parrot," they called. There was no answer. "Aha!" said the dog softly, "Parrot is up to something. She has a plan." Greatly encouraged, he called, "Our leader, Parrot, is not here. We cannot agree to anything until she returns."

Shrew answered, "That's all right. You don't have to agree. Just obey orders."

The two sets of animals settled down on opposite sides of the terrace. CRUMB, in the sun, waited for Parrot's return. As it grew later and hotter they eased their discomfort with hope. Dog kept panting, "Just wait till

Parrot gets back." Lamb, in order to pass the hot weary hours, composed a poem about Cat. He recited it with tears and sweat streaming down his woolly cheeks:

To a Dead Cat

Brave Cat faced the deadly foe
And stoutly fought him, toe to toe.
When blood ran red,
Though others fled,
Cat remained—so Cat is dead.

The other pets were very moved by Lamb's poem.

"If we had all fought as bravely as Cat we would not be in this awful fix."

"Cat died for us."

"Cat did not die in vain. We will follow her example."

"Remember Cat."

66

The thought that each passing hour was bringing victory and revenge closer cheered them. When Parrot returned, inspired by Cat's courage, the Committee to Restore Universal Moral Balance *would* restore universal moral balance. After that they could swim and cool off in the shade.

As ENIGMA sported in the pool and rested on the shady side of the terrace, other wild things in the hot garden took courage and came up too. Bat's relatives skimmed low over the water in full daylight with the swallows, and even the moles came up from underground to splash among the lilies.

Toad and Snake took shelter between two lily pads from the young skunks who were playing a noisy game of water tag. Toad said, "Poor Bat. How he would have loved this."

"Yes," answered Snake, "but it will still be here when he returns."

"Returns!" said Toad.

"Certainly. Don't lose hope."

"Hope! Bat was hung and you talk about hope!" Toad shook his head pityingly. "You must face facts."

"I prefer to think that Bat is alive until I know different."

"You'll never learn. It's a sad day."

The doctor, wide-awake, watched through a window. He wrote without stopping until he completed his final paragraph:

"The politeness shown by my trained animals is unbelievable. They allow the wild things to have the pool and the shade and keep their distance as if they knew that the visitors were timid and easily frightened. The wild animals gain confidence and more and more come. It is a triumph of love."

The doctor then picked up a pair of binoculars and searched the garden. He stopped when he came to the top of the tall oak tree. There was Cat. He went to the phone.

A far-off siren sounded. Dog's ears went up. "It's Parrot!" he said eagerly. "Now we can clear the patio."

When the mole heard this he gathered his family and went back underground. It was cooler there anyway. "Is it all right to eat cutworms again?" he asked Shrew in passing. Shrew nodded. "We won the war."

"Ha!" said Duck from across the pool. "We shall soon see."

The siren grew louder. Many of the wild things left the pool. A fire engine shrieked into the driveway. Out came the doctor to greet the firemen, who had brought a hook and ladder. He pointed to the treetop. They ran the truck alongside and sent a ladder up the tree. A fireman wearing heavy leather gloves climbed it and seized Cat by the scruff. She fought as hard as she could to cling to her branch, but the fireman had a bag in which he put her. He brought Cat down.

Cat rejoined the pets on the terrace. She was very embarrassed. "I could have come down at any time," she explained, "but the air was better up there." The other pets looked away.

"Well, anyway, Parrot will soon be back and then everything will be all right," Duck said.

"Parrot isn't coming back," answered Cat. "She passed me flying south at a mile a minute, screeching 'I'm going back to the Amazon' and cackled till she passed out of sight."

There was nothing to say. Things had never looked worse for CRUMB.

8

Gamal

THE HEAT WAVE CONTINUED. Day after day the sun burned out of a cloudless sky. The sun shower had been the last rain. Even if ENIGMA had wanted to stay on its diet of worms it couldn't. The worms had gone deep underground seeking moisture in the dusty soil. Even the moles couldn't reach them. Slugs had also vanished, as had Japanese beetles, mosquitoes and June bugs. The drought brought hard times for the insect eaters and, had it not been for the food and water on the terrace, many might have died. So they stayed there complaining to each other about the weather and about how dull it was and how nice things used to be back in the dear old garden before the war. The two sets of animals used the pool and the dishes at different times and never spoke. It became very uncomfortable.

Dr. Ordley watched, worked in his laboratory and wrote in his notebook: "There is no doubt that the cause of the bat's high fever is psittacosis. I don't understand what a bat is doing with a bird's disease. Another mystery is what bit the hamster. The poison in the bite is a cobra type. Could there be a small escaped cobra around?" He bent over his microscope.

Shrew had asked some spiders to scout the house for any news of Bat. They went in and out under the door and roamed inside the walls where the hunting was best. The house was an old one and had many dusty corners with a busy insect life. A spider would occasionally come out and report to Shrew, but the reports were all about crickets and powder post beetles. Soon all the spiders were in the house. All the mantises had gone back to the dry garden to feed on grasshoppers, who loved drought

and were about the only insects left there. Shrew and
Snake found their way into the house through a crack.
The spiders were right about the hunting.

Shrew explored upstairs. There, in a small room with
a night light burning, he found shelves and closets
stocked with mysterious jars and boxes. As he scurried
through the dark shadows he suddenly heard his name
called. He whirled about and darted behind a box.
"Who is there?"

"Me. Bat."

"Bat!" Shrew came out of hiding. "We were afraid
you were dead." He was overjoyed. Shrew no longer
thought of Bat as no-account. He remembered Bat's
warning of the attack, Bat's idea about bringing the
Skunks to the rescue, Bat's silly jokes that proved to have
good sense, Bat's success at the newspaper office. Good
old wise reliable steady Bat! They had all misjudged
Bat in the past. Shrew's eyes filled with tears. "What
happened to you?"

Bat said, "Can you get me some June bugs?"

Cold disappointment washed over Shrew. He was
wrong—Bat *was* silly. At such a moment—June bugs!
"What happened to you?" he asked again.

"I don't exactly know. Parrot pushed me off her perch

with a chain around my neck, but that didn't bother me. You can't hang a bat, you know. Our bones are too light. So I just swung there enjoying myself. I saw you all come up on the terrace and when old Parrot got it I laughed so much I guess I passed out. The next thing I knew I was in this cage and the man was putting something nasty down my throat with an eyedropper. I was burning up with fever. Then he gave me some chopped meat and eggs and such glop to eat. Of course, there's no strength in that. If only I could have a good mess of June bugs I could be well enough to get out of here."

Shrew said, "I'll be right back."

After that there was a steady parade of night visitors and Bat recovered quickly. Snake and all the spiders, as well as Shrew, came to see him. Toad said that too many visitors would be tiring and he would wait and see Bat when he got out. The doctor marveled at the pile of legs, wings and shells in Bat's cage. "How does he do it?" He wrote some more about the powers of a bat.

Private Hamster, G. was in the next cage being treated for snakebite. He watched Bat's night visitors come and go and silently noted the steady consumption of insects. One day he cleared his throat. "Ahem—excuse me."

"Yes?" said Bat.

"I couldn't help but notice that you like crickets."

"Just so—so. Not as much as June bugs."

"How do they taste?"

"Something like chicken. Here—try one."

"No thanks. I fancy seeds myself. I was just curious. What else do you like?"

"Oh, lots of things. Moths, mosquitoes, things like that."

"Not blood?"

"Not blood."

"Then you're not a vampire?"

"No. Just a brown bat."

"Oh."

There was a silence. Then Bat asked, "What are you here for?"

"Snakebite."

"Any particular snake?"

"No. It wasn't really a snake at all. It was a shrew, but the doctor says it was a snake."

"Shrew has a rather short temper," said Bat.

"Well, it was in the heat of battle."

"Why did you fight Shrew?"

"I didn't," said the hamster. "I asked if he were a friend or a foe and then he bit me."

"Oh."

"Parrot made us fight. She said that you were all vampires, and that you were the leader. Were you really the leader?"

"We didn't have a leader. We had an organization,
ENIGMA."

"We had an organization too, CRUMB. But we had
a leader, Parrot."

"She made all that stuff up about vampires. None of
it is true."

"No, she didn't make it up. She saw it on TV."

"Then why did you believe her?"

"Well, we hamsters believed her because we agreed
with her. It was bad enough having cats, dogs, lambs,
ducks and parrots all squabbling on the patio. We

didn't want snakes, toads, shrews, skunks and spiders living there too. It would be awful."

"Don't worry about that. They are garden animals— the terrace wouldn't suit them. All they want is to use the pool."

"I don't mind about the pool. I was afraid of a great crowd on the patio."

"I thought you liked crowds. You live in one."

"I get along with them, but I don't like them."

"I don't think that I could get along with them, especially not with Cat."

"The way to get along with Cat is to never, never run from her. If you see her crouch—watch her tail. If the end begins to twitch, just walk straight up to her and tell her that her fur is mussed in back. If she looks really mad, tell her that her nose is running, and offer her a handkerchief. She is bloodthirsty, but she is even more vain, and in no time at all she will be fussing and licking herself."

"That's good to know. How about Dog?"

"Dog is different. He is a blusterer. If you act afraid of him he will be filled with lovely feelings of his own importance which make him so happy that he'll leave you alone."

"Are all hamsters as wise as you are?"

"We have all been raised with a dog and a cat. If we hadn't trained them properly we would have been killed long ago. It's our second nature."

The G in the hamster's name turned out to stand for Gamal. Bat thought the world of him.

Bat finally felt strong and told Shrew it was time to arrange an escape. Shrew brightened at this and began to work on the door of Bat's cage with his clever paws and announced that he could open it. The problem of getting out of the house remained. Bat couldn't squeeze through cracks. He wanted to fly up through a chimney, but doors had to be opened so that he could reach a room with a fireplace. It was very complicated. Shrew and Toad drew maps of the house with carefully worked out schedules of when doors would be open. The day before the escape attempt the doctor took Bat to a window and let him go.

9

Peace

THE DOCTOR WATCHED Bat flutter down from the window. He wrote: "It is remarkable what an effect a bat has. It is no wonder that they are supposed to have magic powers. His appearance on our terrace caused a commotion. All the wild things rushed at him, but fortunately he landed high on the deserted parrot perch safely out of reach. They might otherwise have killed him."

Bat hung head down in the way most comfortable for him and tried to answer the rush of questions one at a time. "No, I didn't fight my way out. He let me go. No, he didn't hurt me. I was sick and he gave me medicine and cured me. He is some kind of a doctor. No thanks, I'm not hungry." He called to the hamsters across the terrace, "Gamal sends regards. He is much better."

The hamsters grew very excited and one called over, "Will he be getting out soon?"

"Traitor," growled the dog. "You are talking to the enemy, and to their leader at that."

"But I only want to find out about Gamal," said one of the hamsters.

Bat pretended to plead with Dog. "Oh, don't hurt him. He is very small and frightened. Please let him come over to hear the news about his brother, who misses him so much and is so sad. He especially asked me to send his love to all his friends and relatives."

Dog looked very fierce and said, "All right, but no tricks." The hamsters looked at each other and one went over to see Bat.

Shrew muttered, "That's not the way to talk to them."

Bat asked that he and the hamster be given a little privacy for a talk.

Shrew said, "No tricks," and scowled and walked off
with the other animals.

When the hamster arrived, Bat and he were alone.
Bat said, "Are you Tawfik?" The hamster nodded.
"Well, don't worry about Gamal. He'll be out soon."

Tawfik asked cautiously, "What did Gamal tell you?"

"Quite a bit. You don't have to worry. We won't
crowd things for you here on the terrace. We really like
the garden better." Tawfik brightened. "Could you get
word around that all we want is to use the pool and

that is enough for us? Let's stop fighting." Tawfik nodded.

"Gamal certainly told you how to handle Dog. Any friend of Gamal is a friend of mine."

"Good," said Bat. "See what you can do."

Tawfik nodded again and went back across the terrace and got very busy whispering to the other hamsters. ENIGMA came back to the parrot perch and Shrew said, "What was that about?"

Bat said, "Aren't you tired of war?"

Shrew said, "We won."

Bat agreed. "We did. Now let's make peace."

"How?"

"Let's have a party."

"I wish you could learn to be serious."

"Do you know a better way to make friends?"

"Friends! With those brutes?"

"Are you so sure that they are all brutes? They think we are vampires out to drink their blood."

"Are you getting soft on pets?"

Here Snake interrupted. "Don't you two start fighting. Peace is what we need, not more fights."

Skunk nodded. "I'm getting tired of standing guard all the time. Let's make peace."

Toad said, "Peace. Let there be peace."

Shrew shrugged. "You're all being fools. I see I'm out-voted—I wash my paws of it. Do whatever you like," and he sulked off to one side.

"Well, let's just arrange a meeting with the pets," said Bat.

Meanwhile the hamsters had been busy. One whispered to Duck, another to Dog. Soon Duck was talking to Cat. Heads were nodding. "Peace." "Agreement." "Life must go on."

When Skunk went over to deliver the invitation to a meeting, the pets were ready. They all gathered around the parrot perch. The doctor in the window wrote rapidly in his notebook.

Bat began the meeting head down on the parrot perch. "Since it is natural for me to hang upside down," he said, "my viewpoint may differ from yours. Still, I think we can all agree that swimming is more fun than fighting, especially in hot weather. Hunting is also more fun than standing guard. So let's take turns swimming and hunting, and avoid crowding each other. All we have to do is agree that CRUMB is as free to hunt in the fields as ENIGMA is, and ENIGMA is as free to use the pool as CRUMB is."

Dog looked surprised. He was ready for harsh terms, but this sounded like a fair treaty. They were offering him something! Cat whispered to him, "It's a trap. Don't accept. Find out more about it first." Dog just shook his head dumbly.

Cat asked Bat, "What do you mean by hunt?"

Bat suggested that they form committees from both sides to look into all such questions and report to the full meeting later on. "Let Snake and Cat settle the question of hunting rules," he said. Everyone agreed, so

Snake and Cat slipped off the terrace into the bushes.

Shrew and Dog were the Rules Committee so they adjourned the meeting till later. For the first time there was mixed bathing in the pool. Shrew and Dog came out much refreshed. They sat down in the shade.

Dog began, "I admired your skill in the battle. It was brilliant."

Shrew looked pleased. "Your plan was excellent. You completely surprised us."

"I see that you are a keen student of war."

They were soon deep in discussion. Shrew was lining up bits of wood. "This is the infantry." He brought in some bigger twigs. "Here is the artillery."

Dog pointed out, "Your flank is exposed."

"Right you are."

When Cat and Snake returned, Dog and Shrew had agreed to have a party. Cat's eyes were shining and there was a feather on her nose.

"Did you make sure that she understood that ENIGMA members were not to be hunted?" Bat asked Snake with a sigh.

Snake nodded. "It's O.K. She is very grateful, but it is going to be hard on the birds. She has tasted blood. Wait until she learns about mice."

"They will have to look after themselves."

The meeting opened with Skunk reading the minutes of the last meeting. Duck moved their adoption. Skunk then said that he had a communication and produced a newspaper. Duck rose to a point of order and asked whom the communication was addressed to. Skunk said it was a news item. Duck then said that it was new business and should be at the end of the meeting. She appealed for a ruling from the chair. Dog roared out, "Read it!" and Skunk opened the paper.

There were three items of interest. The first was about Bat: "The first case on record of parrot fever in bats . . . Unique . . . Scientific curiosity." Everyone applauded. Bat was famous. The second was about a hamster bitten by a cobra. "Small amount of cobra-type venom . . . Be on lookout for escaped cobra . . . Warn children." Shrew was furious.

The third was the most interesting.

"Special Session Hears Bird" read the headline.

"Washington. The special session of Congress called to consider the mid-summer crisis today heard an un-scheduled address by a small green parrot. The bird entered by an open window in the visitor's gallery and perched on the speaker's rostrum while both Houses

were awaiting the arrival of the President. The parrot
warned that vampires were plotting to take over the
country with the help of gullible veterinarians and that
family swimming pools were to be invaded by snakes.

'Sleepers awake!' he cried to considerable applause from the assembled lawmakers.

"The Sergeant-at-Arms failed in an attempt to eject the intruder, who escaped through the same window that he used for entry. The mysterious visitor was last seen flying very rapidly in a southerly direction."

This reading caused a sensation. Dog rose to his feet. "I am, I admit, a little confused. I am, I hope, obedient, trustworthy and, above all, loyal to my leader in the noble cause in which we all fought so bravely, no matter which side we were on. If Parrot seems, now, to be somewhat crazy, all I can do is deeply regret and extend the paw of friendship and anything I can do . . ." Here he broke down and began to sob loudly.

Shrew said, "Three cheers for our brave friend, Colonel Dog!" The loud cheers which followed rose to a positive clamor when the door opened and Gamal ran out to join everyone on the terrace. Dr. Ordley stood in the doorway and watched the celebration.

10

The Rains

THE DOCTOR WROTE in his notebook: "My experiment in peace has been a greater success than I dared hope. Peace is contagious. After I taught the dog and cat to give up violence they were able to tame the wild animals. How? Perhaps we will never understand. The dog plays with a small shrew, the cat with a snake, perhaps the very one that I first saw in the pool. The duck and a handsome skunk are together a lot. Perhaps this is the beginning of a peace epidemic to spread from my garden to all animals everywhere. Will the lion lie down with the lamb? I must make a greater test. For my next experiment I will get a tiger and a grizzly bear."

Late that afternoon they started the party at poolside. ENIGMA brought supplies of grasshoppers, crickets and moths. CRUMB provided soybean paste and dried corn. The party got off to a slow start.

"Have some soybean."

"I've had it. Delicious, but I couldn't eat another bite. Try a cricket."

"Ah yes. Do you eat the legs?"

"Some do, some don't. Here, try a moth."

"Hairy, aren't they?"

"But juicy I think."

No one ate very much and with great relief they decided to go swimming. As it grew later it grew cooler. Some clouds came to darken the sky.

"Looks like rain."

"By the way, what is our new policy on rain?"

"What do you mean?"

No one wanted to refer to the late war, so there was

an awkward pause. Shrew finally said, "I hope the doctor understands that it is to rain on us all alike."

"What do you mean?"

"Do you remember the day that it rained in the garden and not up here?"

"Indeed I do!" said Duck. "Most unfair."

"That is what we thought too. That is why we formed ENIGMA."

"So that it should rain on the patio?" asked Duck.

"Yes."

"How wonderful. Why, we have the same aims. We should have the same organization in that case. One big one instead of two small ones."

Skunk was delighted. "We can draw up new rules satisfactory to all and have elections."

No one else had anything to say, so Duck went on. "I never really liked being a Crumb. We can have a new name. . . ." and she closed her eyes. This time there was no parrot to interrupt her. At last she began to mutter and wave her wings. "E–N–I–G–M–A–C–R–U–M–B. Hmmm . . . Let's mix those initials up a bit." She dipped her webbed foot in the pool and wrote the eleven letters in water on the stone. M–A–N–I–C she wrote, and then U–M–B–R–A–G–E.

Toad said, "Anagrams. I love anagrams. You haven't got two A's."

"So we haven't," said Duck. "How about this—we were two organizations, now we are one. One is our magic number—M–A–G–I–C N–U–M–B–E–R."

"It fits!" cried Toad. "It's an anagram."

At this point everyone began to show a little interest. "What does MAGIC NUMBER stand for?" Snake wanted to know.

Duck proudly answered, "Why, the Moral Associates for General Improvement of Conditions and New Universal Movement for Better Education and Recreation, of course. Now *that's* an organization." Everyone burst into applause. Lamb was particularly thrilled. He was proud to be part of such great events. He began to understand why it was that he was not really a fighter. He was made for other things, higher things, things of the mind. Lamb approached Toad. "You know, you must let me hear your poetry some time." Toad blushed.

Dog, who was still brooding about the rain question, turned to Shrew and asked, "How do you know that Dr. Ordley makes it rain?"

Shrew answered, "If not him, who else?"

Dog nodded. "I guess you are right. It makes sense."

Tawfik, who liked dry weather, asked, "How will the doctor know that we want it to rain on the patio?"

Cat said, "Don't worry. He knows. He knows everything." Cat remembered the electric shocks she had gotten every time she tried to leap at the baby hamster.

"He knows," said Cat again, and went gloomily into her box.

Snake looked at Cat's head sticking up over the top of the box and asked, "What are you doing in there?"

Cat said, "Surely you can understand that at certain times one must visit one's box?"

Snake suddenly realized what Cat was doing and got very embarrassed. "I don't," said Snake.

"You don't what?"

"I don't go to a box."

Cat looked at him curiously. "Where do you go, if not in your box?"

"Oh, just anywhere."

"Just anywhere?" Cat was fascinated. "Can you explain?"

"All right," said Snake. "Come with me." And they went down the steps into the garden and disappeared in a rose thicket. A shower of earth shortly flew out of it and Cat reappeared. "Just anywhere!" she cried wildly, scratching with her back paws. "Just anywhere!" and she crossed the garden in great bounds and leaped the wall into the field.

Dog watched her go. "What is out there?" he asked Shrew.

"Rabbits," said Shrew. "Some quail."

"What are rabbits?"

"Something like hamsters, only faster. They have long ears."

"Faster, hey?"

"Much faster."

Dog got up. The hamsters huddled together in fright but he didn't even look at them. He, too, crossed the garden and leaped the wall. Soon, excited barks and yelps came from the field and Dog could be seen rising and falling in stiff leaps over the tall weeds, with his front paws folded under his chest.

It grew darker. Bat rode in on a freshening breeze. "It looks like rain," he called. "Remember, it now rains on the terrace too. New rules." He sailed up to his knothole.

It suddenly got much darker. The wind began to blow hard and a few large drops made splashes on the warm stones by the pool. Shrew, the hamsters, the spiders, mantises, Toad and Lamb all scurried off to various shelters. Only Skunk and Duck were left.

"Shall we vote to close the meeting?" asked Skunk, looking at the now boiling dark clouds.

"We no longer have enough members for a vote," answered Duck.

"What do the rules say?"

"We don't have a rule yet, and without enough members we can't make a rule." Duck was now stretching her neck up and opening her wings as more of the big drops came down. A white flash of lightning split the sky and the air smelled of ozone as an earth-shaking thunderclap signalled the start of the downpour.

"What shall we do?" asked Skunk, dripping in the blinding rain.

"Why, enjoy it. It's perfect!" cried Duck, flapping her wings in ecstasy.